"The creature did a capering dance."

BEYOND THE SPIDERWICK CHRONICLES

A GIANT PROBLEM

BOOK TWO OF THREE

Tony DiTerlizzi *and* Holly Black

SIMON AND SCHUSTER

London   New York   Sydney   Toronto

First published in Great Britain by Simon & Schuster UK Ltd, 2008
A CBS COMPANY
Originally published in the USA in 2008 by Simon & Schuster Books
for Young Readers, an imprint of Simon & Schuster Children's
Division, New York.
Copyright © by Tony DiTerlizzi and Holly Black, 2008
Book design by Tony DiTerlizzi and Lizzy Bromley.

1 3 5 7 9 10 8 6 4 2

Simon & Schuster UK Ltd
1st Floor, 222 Gray's Inn Road
London WC1X 8HB

A CIP catalogue record for this book
is available from the British Library.

ISBN 978-1-84738-264-1

Printed and bound in Italy by L.E.G.O. S.p.A. – Lavis (TN)

To my grandfather, Harry,
who liked to make up stories.
—H. B.

To all my friends and family back in Florida.
These images of my old home are for you.
—T. D.

Table of Contents

List of Full-Page Illustrations

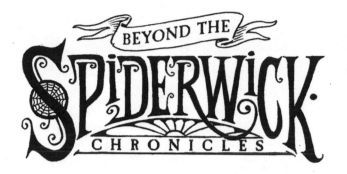

Laurie raised her hand.

Chapter One

IN WHICH Nick and Laurie Get One Lesson and Learn Another

Nicholas Vargas had never been all that good at sports. He liked to play basketball, but he scored a lot higher with a controller in his hand and an animated character shooting the baskets for him. Same with baseball and tennis and even swimming. He saw absolutely no reason why anything would be different when it came to giant-killing.

Nick's stepsister, Laurie, had twisted her blond tangles into braids because she'd read somewhere that it was important to keep hair off your face in a fight. She was determined to learn how to kill giants, but Nick was pretty sure that she was bad at basketball and baseball and swimming both in real life *and* on the screen. A notebook was balanced on her knees and she had set a microcassette recorder on the ground so she could replay the whole lesson later. She chewed the end of her pencil thoughtfully, ready to take extra notes, as Noseeum Jack started to speak.

"First you got to find the giant," he said, sitting down on a stump. They were in the front yard of Jack's ramshackle house in the middle of the day, and the humid air settled on all their shoulders like a heavy blanket. "If he's moving, things have already gone too far. Your best bet is doing the slaying before they wake up."

Laurie raised her hand.

Jack kept on talking. "Couple o' ways to know there are giants underfoot. They like the swamps, but they like freshwater better than salt since they gotta drink it through their skin. Look for rocks and hills, especially if they've got odd-colored grass on 'em. Lots o' the time, that grass is really hair."

Laurie waved her hand a little, impatiently. Nick snatched her pencil. On the page of her notebook, he wrote *HE'S BLIND*.

Jack's eyes were cloudy with what Nick thought might be cataracts. His grandma had had cataracts and the doctors did some kind of laser surgery on them, but Jack's eyes looked much worse than Nick's grandmother's had.

Noseeum Jack. It was a really sad nickname. He'd had the Sight, and blindness took it away from him. Maybe he could see a little bit through the cloudiness, but obviously he couldn't see enough to notice a hand waving in front of his face.

"Are there girl giants?" Laurie asked, interrupting a story Jack had been telling about finding a giant by the way his mountainous head and weedlike hair were covered with dandruff.

"Uh," he said, and then scratched his head. "Sure. I guess. Mostly I never noticed any difference."

Laurie wrote something in her notebook, nodding.

"Look," Nick said. "This is dumb. We're just two kids. And you said that more giants were going to wake up. All of them, maybe. All at once. We can't stop that. This is useless."

"We all got to play the hand we're dealt," Jack said, picking up his machete. "This area's where the highest concentration of giants is. Estimate's maybe thirty still around. There are two good killing blows guaranteed to put down a giant if you just—"

"What hand was I dealt? It's summer," said Nick. "My job in the summer is to have fun. School's out. We shouldn't have to come here every other day."

"But these lessons aren't like school," Laurie said.

"Oh, come on," said Nick. "It's not like you really want to kill anything. You're just excited because you get to talk about giants all day long. This isn't pretend anymore."

She narrowed her eyes. "I know that!"

"Do you?" Nick looked over at Jack, but he was just shaking his head at both of them.

"Wait! I have it!" Laurie said. "We have to get other people to join us."

"That's crazy," Nick said. "No one would believe us."

"We've got to make them believe," said Laurie.

Jack grunted softly. "You think you could?" He looked hopeful, which only made Nick feel more glum. Maybe Jack had already realized what bad students he had and how hopeless this was.

"I know I could," Laurie said, full of stupid certainty. "And we could get Jared and Simon to come back, and maybe they will bring Mallory this time. And maybe they've met other people who would want to help."

"Jared and Simon went home to Maine. They're not coming back," Nick said. "They got what they wanted. They got their uncle's papers."

"Either way," said Jack, "there's one thing we can be sure about: The more people we got to train, the more you both better know. So listen up." With that, he began telling a complicated story about what had appeared to be two giants sleeping side by side, but turned out to be a rare type of giant with two heads.

Laurie recorded every word.

Nick stopped smiling.

Chapter Two

IN WHICH Nick and Laurie Are Surprised by Their Visitor

Nick pressed his finger down harder on the controller, making his car on the screen accelerate. He swerved it in front of Laurie's Volkswagen, knocking into its side and making virtual sparks fly.

She scowled, biting her lip in concentration.

Rockets shot out of her bumper. His car exploded in a whoosh of orange flame as she crowed with laughter. "I'm getting better," she said with a huge smile.

He grinned too. He didn't mind her winning.

CHARLENE VARGAS

He was having fun. The air-conditioning filled the house with cold, sweet air, and just breathing it in made him feel safe. Rain smeared the windows, making the outside blurry and far away. And the more he concentrated on the game, the less he had to think about the nixie waiting in her pond for him to find the rest of her sisters, or all of the giants that might be waking up, or how some blind old guy thought that they could do anything about it. This was how summer was supposed to be.

Besides, this could be considered a kind of training. Maybe. Laurie's reflexes were definitely improving.

Downstairs, a door slammed and his father shouted. "That's not what I said!"

Nick stopped smiling.

"You didn't say

PAUL VARGAS

you would be home early?" Charlene demanded. "You said you would call if something came up. The kids ate hours ago."

"I said I would *try*. The weather, the rain, it's making things hard."

Didn't they realize that just because they

couldn't see anyone else didn't mean they couldn't be heard? His father was a contractor; shouldn't he be aware of vents?

Laurie put down the controller with a sigh, looking at Nick's face. "Everybody fights."

"You tell me everything will be different after the development is done, but there's always going to be another crisis," Charlene yelled. "I don't think you're ready for this. For being married again."

Nick didn't hear the rest because he clapped Jules's headphones over his ears and plugged them into the game. He turned up the sound and set it to single player. He didn't want to hear anyone say anything about his mother. Didn't Charlene know you were supposed to shut up about the dead?

He blew up three of his own cars before Laurie tapped his arm. He shook her off.

"Nick," she said, pulling one side of his headphones down. "Jack's here."

He blinked at her in confusion. "What?" Nick looked around, like Jack was hiding somewhere in the room.

"He's downstairs. Says he has something to show us." She wore a satchel on her hip and had her flip-flops on. "Your dad is freaking out."

"Uh . . ." Nick hadn't even realized she'd left. He took off the headphones and followed her downstairs.

Charlene's back was toward them, her shoulders hunched and shaking slightly as if she were crying. She walked into the study and slammed the door.

Jack stood in the front entrance. He was grinning like a loon.

"Come on, kid," he said. "We got work to do."

"Do you know this man?" asked Nick's dad.

Laurie smiled and started in on one of her elaborate lies. "He's my friend's dad. From where we used to live. Turtle eggs are hatching at the beach and he promised to take us."

"It's very late," Nick's dad said, but he glanced toward the room Charlene was in. Nick bet he wanted to get back to his fight. "Where are you all going? And what did he mean about work?"

"Down to the beach," Laurie said. "My friend Emily is waiting in the car. Her dad thinks we can do a science project about it."

Jack smirked in a way that seemed too amused to be parental.

Nick cleared his throat. "Isn't Jules there? Maybe we can meet up with him."

Jules was always at the beach. It didn't matter if it was sunny or raining, early or late. He could be counted on to surf until his skin

Jack stood in the front entrance.

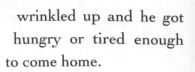

wrinkled up and he got hungry or tired enough to come home.

Nick's dad looked at Noseeum Jack's bare feet and the machete at his hip.

"It's for cutting open fruit," Nick said, following his father's gaze. "And cutting weeds, of course."

"Fruit," repeated his dad. "Fine. Why don't you call your brother?"

"I'll do it." Laurie went to the phone and punched in a bunch of numbers. Then she waited for a few moments, like it was ringing.

"Hi, Jules. It's Laurie. Yeah. No. Um, we were wondering, if we came down to the beach, would it be okay if we hung out with you?

No, we wouldn't have to be really close by or anything. Just so you could see us. We promise not to bother you. Okay. Okay." She put down the phone.

"He says okay," Laurie reported. If Nick hadn't watched her hold the off button on the phone the whole time, even he might have believed she'd really had that conversation.

Nick's dad looked at Noseeum Jack again and sighed. Then he glanced at the study again. "All right. Be back by ten." He pulled his cell phone out of his pocket and handed it to Nick. "Call me if you can't find your brother. Oh, and look out for a raccoon on your way out. Something's been getting into the garbage."

Nick and Laurie walked out onto the lawn with Jack. As the door closed, Nick heard Charlene say something in a shaky voice and his dad shout something back. Thunder cracked overhead, but the rain had slowed to a drizzle.

"Let's go," Jack said.

The lake was choked with newly planted water lilies. Raindrops rippled the water, but there was no sign of the nixie.

"Hey," said Nick, "we promised to help Taloa find the rest of her sisters. Maybe we should—"

"Later! I came to show you both something important, not to dawdle."

"Just one more second," Laurie said. She grabbed a stick of gum out of her bag, chewed it, then used it to affix a piece of paper to the garage door.

Nick watched her as she scrawled on it: JULES—WE SAID WE WERE WITH YOU. DON'T SQUEAL ON US.

"You're crazy! What if they see that?"

She rolled her eyes. "They're going to fight for ages."

"What if one of them storms out?" Ladies on the soap operas his aunt watched did that all the time.

"Into the rain?" Laurie was looking at him like the idea was ridiculous.

"Come on!" said Jack. He made a sweeping gesture with his hands and started walking. They followed him.

The thunder got louder.

Chapter Three

IN WHICH Nick and Laurie Witness One Fight and Almost Have Another

Even with the moon high in the sky and the occasional flashes of lightning, it was spooky to walk through the swampy woods at night. Nick kept putting his foot into sucking mud or getting scratched by a branch he hadn't even seen.

Noseeum Jack seemed to have no trouble, as though he knew the area so well that he no longer needed his eyes to find his way. Maybe it was actually easier for Jack at night, when everyone's sight was as bad as his.

The thunder got louder as they walked through the scrub, eventually growing so loud the ground shook.

"Maybe we should go back," Nick said. "The storm seems to be picking up again."

Jack cackled. "That's no storm."

Just as he said it, something crashed against the earth in a clearing up ahead. Nick ran toward the sound and then stood openmouthed, looking at two giants wrestling in the dirt.

Watching them was like watching hills rise and collide, like watching an earthquake happening in slow motion. Roots and dirt dripped from their broad backs; their fists fell like boulders. One opened a vast maw, and Nick thought he saw dark ivory teeth and a pink tongue, the only signs that the giants were flesh at all.

Mud splashed the nearby trees, covering the bark in a thick, dripping pudding.

"There," said Jack. "What do you think o' that?"

"I think we need to get out of here!" Nick stepped back, but he couldn't seem to tear his gaze away.

With a growl, one of the giants bit into the shoulder of the other. A cry shook the ground. Dust crumbled where flesh should have been and a smell like sulphur filled the air.

Jack was still grinning. "Long as we stay behind these palms and don't make any sudden moves, I'm thinking we're safe enough."

Nick wished that Jack had just said "safe" and not "safe enough." He also wished that Jack could actually *see* how far back they were.

"Why are they fighting?" Laurie asked quietly.

"Territory."

One of the giants—the larger one—rushed

the other, knocking him to the ground and then crashing on top of him like an avalanche. Gouts of mud spattered Nick's face.

"We've got to get out of here," Nick said.

"They wake up too close together sometimes," Jack said. "They want to claim the land around 'em as theirs."

Nick wiped his face, staring, thinking about how when Laurie came, he'd had to move into Jules's room, thinking about how he'd done it without a fight. Good kids were supposed to share.

"I guess that makes sense," Laurie said, but her voice sounded less sure.

It made sense to Nick, but he didn't say so.

The larger giant pummeled the other, smashing the smaller one's head farther into the mud. It followed that with a savage stomp, lifting one foot and bringing it down on the

"Why are they fighting?"

other giant's head, leaving a jagged cut under an eye.

The smaller giant pushed itself up from the ground and lunged. Grabbing the larger one around the middle, it lifted the massive body above its head and hurled it against the ground so hard that nearby trees crumpled from the force. The bigger giant thudded to the ground near where Nick and Laurie stood, branches scraping Jack's back.

Nick screamed. Laurie dug her fingers into his skin. "Shhh!"

When the dust cleared, one giant lay completely still, its body half-crumbled into dirt. The other sagged near it, dark, mudlike blood covering its face.

"Now's our chance," Jack said, like a big tree hadn't almost smashed them flat. "Hear that? It's stilling. We got to go down there and kill it."

Nick looked at the giant, at the rise and fall of its massive chest, at its bent head. "I can't."

"It's hurt," said Laurie, like the giant was a dog with a wounded paw. Her voice shook a little, but her expression was firm.

Jack drew his machete and Nick started talking very fast. "Maybe since it got its territory and it's hurt, if we just leave it alone, it will go back to sleep."

"Right!" Laurie said. "Your prophecy thingy doesn't say how long they stay awake, does it? And that giant looks pretty tired."

"It's not prophecy, it's science," Jack said, but he looked uncomfortable, and Nick was reminded that Jack had seldom, if ever, killed a giant while it was still moving. He'd been going after sleeping giants for years, but sleeping was different.

"Besides, are you sure you can see—"

"I can hear fine," Jack said. "I'll take care o'

the giant. I don't like doing it, but it still's got to be done. You two watch if you want."

Nick tried to think of something that would stop Jack from climbing down next to that hulking, hurting thing and trying to slay it, but there was nothing. Instead, he watched Jack creep closer and raise his machete.

The blade must have caught the moonlight and glittered, or the giant must have heard something, because it turned with a grunt and slapped at Jack, like he was a mosquito that buzzed too close. That slap sent Jack sprawling back toward them, his leg bent at an odd angle and his head knocking hard against the ground. The machete flew out of his hands, clanging against wood.

"Jack," Nick whispered, starting toward him.

"Wait," said Laurie, grabbing his arm. She was watching the giant, but it didn't seem to be paying them any attention.

Nick shook her loose and ran over to him. "Jack!" he said louder, not caring about anything except finding out if Jack was okay.

Jack moaned a little and pushed himself into a sitting position with a wince. He looked around like he was confused.

"Can you stand up?" Nick asked him.

"I don't know," he said.

"Lean on me," Nick said.

Laurie scurried to get the machete and came back with a long stick. They

helped him up, and, between the stick and Nicholas, Jack was able to stagger out of the clearing. Even as thin as Jack was, his weight was heavy on Nick's shoulder. He stepped carefully through the dark as Laurie ran ahead with the machete, clearing the way of branches and making sure they weren't about to step into a hole or trip on a bush. Even still, Nick stumbled twice on the way to Jack's ramshackle house.

Jack watched them with his cloudy eyes

and grunted when his bad leg hit something, but he didn't say anything — not about giants, or even doctors — and shook his head when they wanted to call an ambulance. They settled him in a threadbare chair, and Laurie tried to get his legs propped onto a low stool.

Nick walked into the kitchen, getting a package of frozen peas out of the icebox. That's what his mom had put on his arm years ago when she'd been afraid he'd broken it.

Walking back into the living room, Nick accidentally knocked his hip into a cabinet. A bunch of papers slid to the floor. Dropping the peas, he picked up the papers and was about to shove them back on top when he got a better look at them: a yellowed diploma from a university and an old picture of a young Jack with his arm slung around a pretty girl. He was grinning like he'd just won the lottery.

Nick picked up the peas.

In the living room Laurie was adjusting the rabbit ears on the television, as if the fuzz would coalesce into a picture. Nick put the peas against Jack's thin leg where the scrapes looked particularly raw.

"It's getting late," Jack said. His voice sounded hoarse and tired. "You two should get on home."

As they were saying good-bye and asking again if there was anything they could do, Nick realized that Jack was old.

Nick had known that, but he'd never really thought about what it meant. Now he couldn't get the thought out of his head.

When Nick and Laurie got home, they found Jules sitting on the hood of his car, his calves and feet coated with sand, nodding in time with music coming from his tiny earbuds.

"You waited!" Laurie went up to Jules and put her arms around his waist, startling him out of his musical fugue. "You're the best!"

He pulled off the earbuds. "Where were you guys? Aren't you too young to start sneaking around?"

"Mom and your dad were fighting," Laurie said, and a lie wouldn't have shocked Nick as much as her use of the truth did.

"About what?" Jules asked.

"I don't know," she said. "It was just really upsetting. We went for a walk." Laurie smiled and continued on blithely. "Nick bought me an ice cream."

Jules looked at Nick like he didn't know

him. "Uh, that was cool of you."

Nick thought that Laurie had finally gone too far and that there was no way Jules was going to swallow any of this, especially the part about Nick being nice. Maybe Laurie thought that too, because she reached into her pocket and pulled out a key chain. A heart-shaped piece of cork with a clear plastic center and something inside of that.

"Here, I've been meaning to give this to you, Jules. I made it. For luck. See, it can even go in the water."

"Thanks." Jules looked at it blankly and then slid it onto his key ring. "You really made this for me?"

She nodded.

Pushing off the car with a grin, he ruffled her hair as he walked past them and toward the house.

"What?" she said when she saw Nick's expression. "I told you I always wanted a brother."

The creature did a capering dance.

Chapter Four

IN WHICH a Sandspur Gets Stuck with Nick

All night the rain came down, and Nick tossed and turned on his bed. Jules slept peacefully on the other side of the room, oblivious to the distant thunderous bellowing that Nick couldn't help thinking was giants awakening and stretching their lungs like newborns.

Around his side of the room were models of ships and planes he'd carefully made with glue and tweezers and balsa wood. The Viking ship kit that his mother had given him was finally finished and resting beside the others. But now they looked the way he imagined that he might look to a giant—fragile. Nick closed his eyes tightly, but nothing he thought of shut out his fears.

He woke early the next morning and went downstairs to pour himself cereal. Eating mechanically, he chewed without actually tasting the food. He couldn't stop thinking about the way the giant had knocked Jack down like he was made of paper. Surely now Jack would see that training Nick and Laurie to fight these things was a joke.

Maybe Jack could find some hero kids. Like from books. Like Jared. He thought about calling the phone number Jared had given them when he left and asking for advice, but he was afraid that all of Jared's advice would be as crazy as Jack's was.

Out of the corner of his eye Nick saw something dart across the lawn. He walked over to the door and saw a creature the size of a large cat sprinting away on three-toed feet. Yesterday's garbage was scattered across the grass.

Nick opened the door. "Hey!" he called.

The creature stopped and looked back with golden eyes. It was very small, covered in a dusting of tan fur all the way down to its three-toed feet, and was staring at him with an almost comical expression of astonishment.

Nick started toward it, but as one foot hit the first of the brick steps, the other slammed onto a bowl of milk. It cracked under his weight, splinters of pottery slicing his flip-flop. He fell on the walkway, skinning his hands on the cement.

He knew exactly who had left that bowl there.

"Laurie!" he shouted. *"Laurie!"*

His palms were streaked with gravel and blood. He felt stupid and angry and then

embarrassed when tears stung his eyes. Blinking them back, he took a shaky breath and waited for his hands to stop throbbing.

Laurie stuck her head out past the screen door. She was wearing pajamas with cats on them. "What happened? I heard you yelling," she said with a yawn.

"You left out your cereal bowl. What does it look like happened?"

"Oh," she said. "That was for the faeries." She stared at him a moment longer. "You *stepped* in their milk?"

Just then Charlene pushed the door wide. She was hastily tying her robe. "Go get me some hydrogen peroxide," she told Laurie, looking at Nick's hands.

"I don't know where that is," Laurie complained.

"I'm fine." Nick got up and walked a few paces toward the street. He didn't want his new stepmother taking care of him like he was a baby.

Charlene sighed and rubbed her face. "You two, stay right there. I'll get it myself."

"Sorry about your foot," Laurie said.

He shrugged, although he wanted to yell at her. Just not when Charlene would be back any second and would probably take Laurie's side. "I saw that little faerie again. The one that filled Dad's car with sand. I think he's been at the garbage."

"Maybe we can make friends with it."

"Don't we have enough problems with the

faeries we've already befriended?" Nick looked over at Taloa's lake.

She looked toward the lake then too. "Hey," Laurie said. "What's that?"

He squinted. The three-toed creature seemed to be lifting up tiny pieces of something and tossing them around. A few floated on the water. "There it is!"

Charlene stepped into the doorway, holding a brown bottle. "Nick, come here."

He glanced back at her. "I'm okay," he said absently, turning to the lake. "My hands are fine."

"You can keep hating me," she called to him. "Just let me put a Band-Aid on your scrape."

His face reddened. He didn't *hate* her. It wasn't that.

"We'll be right back," Laurie said. "Nick and I need to talk."

Charlene stared at Laurie as if stunned, and then her shoulders sagged. "Sure, okay," she said softly, putting the bottle on the stoop. "I'll leave the medicine here in case you change your mind."

Laurie was already walking toward the lake, and Nick ran to catch up to her.

As they got close, the creature did a capering dance. They could see a few tattered pieces of a tabloid magazine were pressed in the wet dirt, rocks holding them in place. The creature hissed at them and kicked aside a rock, snatching up the scrap of paper in one hand. A few more scraps floated on the lake. Nick looked at what remained of the message:

I E K MY S S E R S A O N
YOU I L L B E S R Y

"Hey!" Nick darted toward the creature, trying to snatch the piece of paper.

"Do *you* think Taloa left us this message?" Laurie asked.

The thing leaped out of Nick's way and then shoved the paper in its mouth.

"*I* think Taloa left us the message," Laurie said.

"Great," said Nick. "Do something."

The creature went very still. For a moment Nick didn't understand what was happening, and then he realized that the creature didn't seem to know they could see it. It didn't know they had the Sight.

Nick looked away from it and tried to edge up without seeming to. But before he could take more than a couple of steps, Laurie threw herself into the mud, tackling it.

The creature bleated horribly and spat out the letter. It was an *S*.

"Get something! Anything!" Laurie shouted, trying to keep the tiny body from squirming out of her grasp.

"Off! Off! Off!" the creature wailed.

Nick sped off to the house and looked in the garage, tearing apart the boxes from when Laurie and her mother had moved in and the old stuff Nick, Jules, and their dad had moved out to make room for them. And there, in the back, were boxes with Nick's mother's name on them. He walked toward them slowly and lifted one of the flaps. A wig she'd worn when she was really sick was at the top. He stared at the strands of hair for a long moment, then looked away and kicked the box savagely. His foot made a dent in the side. Turning away, his gaze fell on a large plastic birdcage among the boxes. The inside was filled with plastic flowers and a bird made with turkey feathers that he remembered helping to glue together. The faerie monster thing might fit in the cage, but it'd be a tight squeeze, and the whole thing didn't look very sturdy.

He picked it up and dumped out the flowers and fake bird, but as he was heading out he saw a box from Laurie's house. CAT STUFF. He hadn't even known they'd had a cat.

Setting down the cage, he ripped off the tape. Inside he found a cat bed, several bowls, a half-empty bag of litter, and a leash. The blue nylon leash was the kind that fit around the cat's whole body. Nick looked at it and grinned.

He ran back, holding up both.

"The cage!" Laurie yelled, and tried to force the flailing and shouting thing into it.

A moment later, when it was inside and chewing on the bars, she slumped down in the dirt. "You sure took your time," she said.

He grinned, looking at her bedraggled pajamas and muddy hair. He didn't feel so resentful about stepping on the cereal bowl anymore. "You said you wanted to befriend it. I was just giving you the time you needed."

Laurie stuck out her tongue.

The creature wailed. "How did you see me? Oh! No! How? How could I not see that you see?" it said, wrapping thin arms around its plump body.

"Maybe we should figure out what the note is supposed to say," said Nick, gesturing toward the remaining rocks and scraps of magazines.

Laurie was too busy staring through the bars

at the creature to notice. "What's your name, little guy?" she asked.

It just hissed at her.

"I'm going to call you Sandspur," she said rapturously.

It made a strange, gibbering noise.

"You like your name, don't you?" she asked.

"Did you get the paper it was holding?" Nick asked her. He didn't think the creature liked its name all that much. That hadn't seemed like a happy sound.

"Here." She handed him the crumpled and wet wad. He waded into the lake, grabbing for the rest of the letters, heedless of the way his knee and palms stung when the water hit them. He got bits of magazines that read *E*, *O*, *E*, *W*, *I*, *S*, *R*, and *T*. One piece still seemed to be missing, but he couldn't find it.

"Huh," Nick said. He looked at the message

again. "You" looked complete and the word next to it could be "will" using the *W*.

"'You will,'" he read.

"I will what?" asked Laurie, not paying attention.

"'You will be sorry'!" said Nick.

"I'll be sorry? For what? I *already* apologized that you tripped! Why do you always have to—"

"No, no," he said, interrupting her and pointing to the letters. He started to set the papers he'd found homes for in their places. "That's what the last four words say."

Laurie pointed. "That there could be 'sisters.'"

"So we have: 'I e k my sisters a on you will be sorry.'"

"Whatever it says, it doesn't sound good."

"'I seek my sisters alone,'" Nick read, moving the last of the letters around. "'You will be sorry.'"

"Oh no." Laurie stood up. "She's right. We should have gone out more. What if something happens to Taloa now? It will be because of us."

"We didn't have any idea where to look," Nick said, but he felt ashamed. They'd looked halfheartedly in the beginning, but they should have kept at it instead of going to giant-killing lessons he knew were useless. Laurie had stopped insisting about Taloa, and Nick had blown the whole thing off.

Charlene's hair was wet and she cradled a cup of coffee in both hands when Nick and Laurie walked in. Nick's father was pouring himself a travel mug full of orange juice. He took one look at Laurie in her muddy pajamas and started to laugh. Nick, who had been waiting to get scolded, was relieved.

"What game were you two playing?" Charlene asked.

"We fought giants," Laurie said with a huge grin, holding up what must have looked like an empty birdcage. "And I caught a faerie."

"You think you two will be okay until Jules gets back from the beach?" Charlene asked. "Paul's headed to the office to drop some stuff off, and I'm going to the grocery store."

"We'll be fine," Nick said.

She looked at him, and Nick thought she seemed sad. "Put some antiseptic on your cuts, okay, Nicholas?"

He nodded. He wanted to tell her that he didn't hate her, but he couldn't find the right words.

Also, if she and his dad were going to get a divorce, then maybe he did hate her.

Or at least, he wanted to reserve the right to.

He went up to Laurie's room and flopped on the bed, looking at the caged goblin thing while she took a shower. He tried to find a drawing of something like it in *Arthur Spiderwick's Field Guide to the Fantastical World Around You*, but none of the pictures were quite right.

"Let me out," said the little creature beseechingly.

Nick regarded it for a moment and then shook his head.

"Pleeeeeease." Its voice was a thin whine. "You are big and powerful, but I am tiny and useless. Let me go."

"Why were you even hanging around here? Eating our trash? Don't you have someplace better to be?"

"So many giants. All their territory is big and I am small. Nowhere left to come but here. Too many!"

"How many?" Nick asked nervously.

But the little creature yowled

instead of answering. "Please! Please! Please! LET GO!"

"I think Laurie just wants to feed you lots of cookies and dress you up in doll clothes," Nick said. "I don't think it'll be that bad."

Laurie came in at that moment, toweling off her hair.

"Does it ever bother you?" Nick asked. "Lying like you do?"

"I wasn't lying to my mom," she said.

Nick sighed. "Fine. Whatever. You didn't *technically* lie *that* time, okay?"

Laurie looked at her chipped toenail polish and leaned down to pick at it. "I like making things up. I'm good at it."

Nick didn't say anything. After all, most of the lies she'd told had been to get both of them out of trouble.

"At the last place we lived I used to tell

people that I spent all these weekends with my dad. Even though all I have is the picture I showed you; I haven't seen him or heard his voice in years. I would say that he took me all these places. Disneyland. Antarctica. That he had bought me a pony named Rosie and kept it at a stable near his place so I could ride her when I stayed over. The hardest thing was remembering all the lies I told."

Nick had no idea how to respond. He had figured that Laurie had been lucky her whole life and he was the unlucky one, but now he wasn't sure.

"After a while, I could tell that they didn't believe me. Even my friends. But then your dad picked me up from school, and he's got a fancy car just like I said, and he takes me places. Just like I said. Like my lies came true."

"That's why you were okay with taking our

last name? Because you wanted my dad to be your dad." Nick narrowed his eyes at her.

Laurie shrugged her shoulders. "I guess I keep thinking that after everything, lying worked. Lying works."

The smell of smoke was the first thing Nick noticed. He was watching Laurie try to get the hobgoblin—because that was what she'd decided he was—to eat. She had somehow gotten him into the cat harness and set out an array of foods on a plate. First she stabbed a wedge of cheese with a chopstick and put it up to his mouth. Then she tried a dripping blob of peanut butter. The hobgoblin turned up his nose at each of the offerings. The only thing Sandspur seemed interested in chewing on was his leash.

"Did you leave the oven on?" Nick asked. "Are you cooking pizza bites for this thing?"

"That's a great idea," she said, standing up.

Then he heard a massive crack and a boom so physical that it seemed sonic. The room shook. They raced to the window in time to see one of the half-built houses in the development collapse. The development that Nick's dad had planned on their kitchen table. The development where they were standing. The smell of smoke was overwhelming now.

The hobgoblin howled.

"What do we do?" Laurie shouted.

Out the window Nick watched as two giants crashed together through the houses, blowing hot breaths of flame. He recognized one and felt cold dread settle at the pit of his stomach. He had a scar under his eye. It was the one they had left alive.

"The whole house will come down on us! We have to move!" Laurie shouted.

They ran out into the hallway and saw Jules stumble up the stairs, wiping his eyes.

"What's going on?" Jules sounded panicked.

"We've got to get out of here," said Nick.

With Laurie cradling the hobgoblin to her chest, they ran down. Jules threw open the front door.

One of the giants had fallen into a row of houses. Their faux chimneys were still raining bricks and their siding shredding under his weight. Sparks had caught on wood and were starting to burn. A cloud of dust choked Nicholas.

"Come on!" Nick shouted, grabbing Laurie's arm and racing out into the street.

"We need a plan," she yelled.

"This *is* my plan!" he shouted back. The hobgoblin was still howling, sliding around

"Come on!"

in her arms and clawing at her shirt.

Then, screeching into reverse, his brother's car, surfboards on top, came to a halt in front of them.

"Get in, idiots!" Jules shouted, and Laurie scrambled inside while Nick stared at Jules. What did Jules see? How could they explain what was happening?

Laurie pulled on Nick's arm, and he sprang to life, throwing himself onto the backseat and holding on as Jules stepped on the gas so hard the door slammed closed all by itself.

A load of lumber and cement blocks rained down near the car, several boards and a chunk of cement slamming onto the roof and trunk of the car. The ceiling dented hard enough that it pocked down at Nick and Laurie. He screamed and Laurie gasped.

Jules looked back at him in the rearview

mirror. "I think you have a lot to explain."

"Us? You mean you can see them?" Nick asked.

"What?" Jules asked. "Those megamonsters? Of course I can see them. They're like a hundred feet tall!"

As Nick tried to absorb the shock of that, he glanced back. Through the rear windshield, his whole world was on fire.

"I saw this thing underwater today."

Chapter Five

IN WHICH Noseeum Jack Is Seen

They swerved off the road and screeched into the parking lot of a strip mall. Nick looked out the windshield at the steaming hood and then down at his shaking hands. People walked past to their cars as though nothing was wrong. A few turned toward the cloud of black smoke in the sky, but most didn't even seem to notice.

"Are you okay?" Jules asked, not looking at either of them. He seemed to be staring at nothing.

"Yeah," Nick and Laurie said softly.

"And that thing you have with you? It's fine too?"

"It's fine," Laurie said, cuddling Sandspur. He made a small noise but didn't struggle to get away from her.

Jules opened the door and got out, walking down the side of his car, his fingers trailing numbly over the surface. Nick climbed out too, Laurie shuffling out behind him.

The whole back bumper was missing and the trunk had been crushed on one end, the metal low enough to drag and spark when the car moved. Jules's surfboard was gone.

"Is that what you two have been so secretive about?" Jules asked, his voice sounding like their dad's. "You two knew about this? About those monsters? *How?*"

For a moment the three of them just looked at one another, breathing hard.

"One of her books. It's about faeries and how to see them. Like the giants. And other stuff," Nick finished lamely, since Jules was staring at him like he'd grown a second head.

"I saw this thing underwater today," Jules said. "It had a tail like a fish and claws and sharp teeth. As soon as it saw me looking at it, it grabbed me and pulled me down underwater. I started thrashing around, not being able to breathe, and finally I kicked free. Did that have to do with—"

"I don't understand," Nick said. "How did you get the Sight?"

"The sight? What's the sight? Do you mean *seeing*? Because I'm pretty sure I could always do that," said Jules.

Nick shook his head. "The Sight is the ability to see all kinds of weird stuff that actually exists but you wish didn't."

"It's magic," said Laurie.

"Okay, explain that better. What am I seeing and why am I seeing it?"

"Were you swimming in the pond here in the development?"

"That mud hole? No way."

"Well, did you do *anything* differently? Find anything odd? What did you have on you?"

"Nothing. I was surfing. Keys, I guess."

"Keys?"

"I keep them on a lanyard in my trunks. The area's too sketchy to just shove them up under the hood. And then I can lock my cell in the car."

Nick felt a prickle of dread. "Let me see."

Jules shrugged and held out his key chain. It had a cork heart attached to it, with clear plastic in the center. Laurie had given it to Jules the day before. And as Nick held it up to the light, he saw that it held a perfect four-leaf clover in the center.

"This," Nick said. "This is why."

Nick looked over at Laurie and noticed something. Her locket was around her neck. The one she'd lost. The one that had the clover he'd found inside of it. "How could you?" His voice sounded rough.

Laurie's eyes went wide and frightened. "You agreed that we should let people know."

"Not like this." Nick took a step toward her, not sure what he was going to say or do.

At that moment Jules's phone rang.

"Dad," Jules said, flipping it open. "The house. The houses—Oh, you know? Yeah. We're okay.

67

We got out in time. No, we're in front of Big Bad Pizza. You know, by the video store.

"Yeah, okay.

"No, I don't know where Charlene is." His voice rose in panic and he looked toward Nick and Laurie.

Nick shook his head and mouthed "store" at the same time Laurie nodded.

"She's okay," Jules said into the phone. "She wasn't at the house."

"Me too. Bye, Dad." He hung up. "Why didn't you tell me any of this was going on?"

"Why didn't you tell Dad?" Nick asked. "It's not so easy, is it?"

Jules sighed and ran a hand over his face. "He wants us to come over to Sunpalm Hotel by the library. He says not to worry."

Laurie frowned. "That's because he has no idea what he should worry about."

Their two rooms in the Sunpalm Hotel were next to each other, with a door joining them. As usual, Laurie got a whole bed to herself in the kid's room, while Jules and Nick were going to have to fight over the covers in the other double bed.

Nick's dad was already in the parent's room, pacing and making phone calls. He had barely noticed them when they'd knocked, opening the door, pointing to their room, unlocking it with a key card, and then putting the key card in Jules's hand.

They flung themselves down on the beds, and Laurie tied Sandspur's leash to the exposed pipe under the sink in their bathroom. The hobgoblin immediately started teething on his tether.

Charlene opened the door between the rooms about a half hour later, holding a bag of groceries.

She looked pale and tired. Nick's dad was getting up to leave. He gave her a hug, pressing his face into her neck, and then headed out.

"Where's he going?" Nick asked.

"The police want to talk to him," Charlene said softly.

Nick's dad didn't come back until late afternoon. When he did, he picked up a piece of cold chicken and sat down on the bed next to Nick and Laurie. His untucked shirt was smeared with grime and his eyes were red-rimmed. Dirt streaked his cheekbone.

"You didn't see anyone hanging around, right? That level of destruction—I just can't believe it. The houses are still burning, and one of the fire engines somehow got crushed. From debris. I'm not sure."

Nick shook his head, but he didn't know how to answer. He looked at Laurie.

"That old guy?" Nick's dad held up his hands in mock surrender. "I know you said you knew him, Laurie, but he looked homeless to me. I said something about him to the police, and they said they've heard some weird stories about him too. Now, that doesn't mean anything, but if you know something, you have to tell me, okay?"

"We don't know anything," Laurie said, but her voice hitched when she said it.

"Paul," Charlene said. "Come have some more food."

He turned toward Charlene, and Nick braced himself for his dad to ask the right question, or for Charlene to realize that she didn't know Noseeum Jack and for Laurie's lie to start unraveling, but Nick's dad said nothing. He just held out his hand for the plate.

They watched television with the door between the two rooms closed for about an hour. Finally Laurie stood up as though she'd been thinking about it for a while. "We have to sneak out," she said. "We have to find Noseeum Jack. Jack will know what to do."

"Noseeum Jack?" Jules asked. "What kind of name is that?"

"He used to slay giants."

"Used to?"

"He's blind now. But he had the Sight and knows how to kill them. He'll know what to do about this."

"He hurt his leg recently too," Nick put in with a glare in Laurie's direction. She should never have given Jules the Sight.

Jules looked at them both skeptically but picked up his keys off the dresser. "Okay," he said. "Let's go. Quick. Before Dad and your mom start thinking about dinner."

"What about Sandspur?" Nick asked.

Laurie looked in the bathroom. "It's okay. We can leave him. He's asleep on the bath mat."

A black man leaned against a gunmetal gray sedan in the driveway, one gloved hand picking at a speck of lint on his suit. He looked like a lawyer, and Nick felt guilty, thinking about the kind of trouble that would make Jack hire one who was so fancy.

Was it about the development? Did the police really think that Jack had something to do with it? Who wore leather gloves in Florida? Maybe

he was with the FBI? CIA? Maybe he was even a member of a paranormal investigation squad. Then they could take all of this out of his hands.

"I'll be right back," Nick told Jules and Laurie as he climbed out of the car.

"Hey!" Jules said. "I'm going with you."

"Please," Nick said. "I can't explain everything right now." He looked at Laurie, who must have sensed what he was going to say because she was already scowling. "She can tell you lots while I'm gone."

"You better get back before she's done," Jules said as Nick shut the door.

The man saw Nick crossing toward the house and smiled. "You looking for my dad?" he asked.

"Your . . . dad?" For a moment Nick couldn't understand what the man meant. Then he realized. Jack. Jack had a son who wore pinstriped suits and shiny shoes. Jack had a son

who looked like an FBI
agent.

"Yeah," Nick
said finally. "Is he
home?"

The man smiled
again. "He's been
getting you pulled
into his stories,
hasn't he? Got
you stabbing rocks
and hills, telling
you they're giants. I
remember how magical
it all seemed. Like we were
heroes. You feel something like that?"

"But there *are* giants," Nick said, dumb-
founded. How could Noseeum Jack's own son
not have the Sight?

The man tousled Nick's hair. "It all seems

JACK JUNIOR

really real when he describes it, doesn't it?"

He looked up into the man's kind brown eyes and felt a chill pass through him. "How come you're here? Where's Jack?"

"You probably noticed Dad can't see too well anymore. He's been insisting that he does all right on his own, but we — my wife and I — well, we don't think he's managing as well as he says. He's coming to live with us."

"But the giants," Nick sputtered. "They're waking up. All of them."

"I heard. Like cicadas, right?"

"You don't understand." Nick wanted to scream in the man's face, but he kept his voice as polite as he could make it. "It's true. I've seen them."

The front door of the house opened and Jack walked out, leaning heavily on a cane. Seeing him look so frail filled Nick with despair.

Jack's son shook his head. "You need to go back home. Especially if you believe his stories.

Imagine how dangerous giants would really be? You can't do anything about something like that."

Scowling, Nick ran over to where Jack was shuffling across the lawn. "You were right," he said. "The giant. We should have stopped it. It came back and it set fire to everything. All the houses. And now we don't know what to do."

Jack blinked his cloudy eyes a few times. "I'm glad you and your sister are all right. I left something for you in the back. Something you were thinkin' on.

"Tried to do some research, too, after our last talk. About how long giants stay awake. There seems to be something that they're here to do, something that they can't rest until they accomplish. At first I thought they had to kill each other, take over all the territory, but I don't think it's that. Jared took some of the notes I needed, and I can barely see the rest even with the biggest magnifying glass I got, but it looks like

"There's something they hunt."

there's something they hunt. Here." He thrust a few sheets of paper into Nicholas's hands.

Nick looked down and saw a drawing of giants blowing flames at dark pools of mud. Some of the pools seemed to have lizard heads in them. Maybe they were alligators? "Wait. Aren't you going to be helping us?"

"I'm sorry, Nick."

"No. Wait. We'll do whatever you say. We'll learn!"

"I'm too old," Jack said. "And you're too young. I'm sorry about your house, but I think that maybe it's the best thing. Lie low. Get as far away from here as you can."

"Jack!" Nick said, his voice cracking with anguish. But Jack was walking toward his son, and Nick had no more words with which to call him back.

Not sure what to expect

Chapter Six

IN WHICH Nick Finds Hope in Wreckage

Nick turned the corner to the back of Jack's house, not sure what to expect. All he saw, though, was a kiddie pool, its surface covered in a thick layer of slime. Nick looked down into the green sludge as though he could figure out some kind of answer there.

But Jack had given up, and even his last present was stupid. Maybe he thought they could clean it out and go swimming.

Nick kicked the side and watched the water slosh, then walked back to the car. He slid into the backseat with a shake of his head.

"I don't understand," Laurie said. "Who's that guy?"

"Just drive," Nick said. He handed her the papers. "It's over."

Jules pulled the car away from the curb, ignoring the grate of metal on road.

Laurie unhooked her seat belt and turned around. "What do you mean? Nick!"

"Jack's leaving. He's giving up. He says we should give up too."

The car banged into a steep hole and ground hard.

Laurie nearly fell into the backseat. "How do we give up?" she shouted at Nick. "He said all of Florida is going to burn!"

"Hey," Jules said. "I'm driving here!" He hit the gas, but the wheel just spun.

Jules got out and walked around the car. "Nick, come help me," he called.

Nick slid out of the backseat and leaned down to look at the pothole. The more he looked at it, though, the more it looked like the beginning of a *sinkhole*. Muddy water pooled along with chunks of fallen asphalt in the pit. He'd seen them before, but never on a road; they didn't happen *that* fast.

"Weird," Nick said.

"Forget about staring at it. There's some lumber by that guy's garbage. Grab it and we'll see if we can make a ramp to get the tire out."

They shoved a plank into the hole, and when Jules pushed the gas again, this time the car moved forward and away from the ramshackle house, the gross kiddie pool, and any hope of someone to tell Nick what to do.

The worst part was that he knew he hadn't really taken Jack seriously. Nick had wanted to give up. He'd figured that someone else could handle things. Now he still had no idea what to do, but he was afraid there really was no one else. His stomach hurt.

That night in the hotel room, Nick couldn't sleep. He looked through the books that Laurie had shoved into her backpack. First, he flipped idly through *Arthur Spiderwick's Field Guide*, staring at the pictures of giants. There was nothing new there.

He picked up another book. Fairy tales. Princes. Princesses. Nothing that seemed like it would help.

He thought about when he'd met the people who had put the guide together and about what the woman had said to him. Fairy tales about giants. But what did reading a story about a

Overleaf
Area newspaper coverage
of Mangrove Hollow fire

Mangrove Hollow Fire Considered Suspicious

BY MARIE FRANCIS, STAFF REPORTER

Photo © Chris Collura/SKY-CHASER.COM

Mangrove Hollow fire as seen from Durrwachter Drive.

East Coast, Florida. — According to local authorities, a fire that started early yesterday morning in the newly developed subdivision of Mangrove Hollow has been brought under control. The blaze was extinguished by county firefighters, but only after flames had destroyed dozens of new homes, many of which had just been completed and approved for occupancy.

Mangrove Hollow's developer and builder, Paul Vargas, and his family were the only residents residing in the development at the time of the fire. They have been evacuated from their home. Mr. Vargas could not be reached for further comment.

There are no reported injuries at this time.

The fire is believed to have started in a pile of leaves and brush located on the Mangrove Hollow site. But officials also were trying to confirm reports that a man was seen running from the woods a short time before the fire was reported.

Fire Chief Rick Richter said, "The fire appears to be suspicious because we do not think weather played a factor in starting the blaze." He continued, "Although there have been a record number of brush fires across the county, the area weather does not appear to be a contributing factor as an ignition source."

The city's head arson investigator, Detective Lizzy Bromley, interviewed several area residents seeking information on any suspicious activities that might be relevant to the case. "Everyone seems just shocked by the level of devastation," she responded when asked for a comment. "One veteran said it sounded like being in a war zone."

Firefighters were plagued by uncharacteristically stiff winds, which contributed to the difficulty in battling the flames. Several pieces of fire apparatus, including the department's main pumper, were crushed by falling debris.

tailor or whatever have to do with this?

His flipping stopped on the Pied Piper of Hamelin, and Nick stared at the page. The illustration showed a picture of a piper followed by a sea of rats, no giants in sight. Rats, lured by the sound of his music.

Then the rats disappeared but the town didn't pay up, and the piper lured the kids the same way he did the rats.

With the pipe. With music. Like Taloa had lured the giant. But, of course, Taloa was gone, and with her, any luring.

Maybe he could find Taloa. Or her sisters, if she hadn't found them already. He groaned. He had no idea where to even begin to look.

At his groan, Jules rolled over in his sleep and scratched his nose.

Then Nick did remember something from the field guide. He flipped frantically to the page. Mermaids. Better than nixies at luring people with their song. Maybe they would be better at luring giants, too. Away from houses that could be burned and people who could be stomped. Away.

Nick wondered if it could be possible. Just the thought filled him with a sick excitement.

The next day Nick's dad loaded them into the car and they drove to Mangrove Hollow. Fire had blackened the lawns, and in one place the pavement was cracked in a circle as though some massive thing had crashed into the center of it.

The boulders were still where they had been hurled, one crushing a newly planted tree.

But the worst thing was seeing the houses. No

longer promising a neighborhood full of kids and fun, no longer promising the fulfillment of his parents' dream, no longer promising anything.

"It's not so bad," said Nick's dad faintly.

"Insurance will cover it," Charlene said, putting her hand on his arm.

"Some of it, anyway," he said, his voice so low that Nick had to strain to hear him.

Their house was even worse. Not burned like most of the others, but collapsed, one side slumped into a pile of shingles and the other stripped to beams. Clothes, furniture, and other familiar things stuck out from the piles of wallboard.

Nick waded through the debris. It was hard to balance on things, but he was determined to find something. Something that was his.

"Get away from there," said his dad.

"Just a second," he called, staring at the shards of televisions, the bent metal of his dad's exercise equipment. He thought of the boxes of his mother's things, buried deep in the rubble of the garage. He thought of stupid stuff—the ugly clay ashtray he'd made for his dad, the pictures of him with his classes, a stuffed rabbit that Jules used to sleep with and had given to him and he had kept under his bed.

"Come back!" his dad yelled. "That's dangerous."

Nick knew he should go back, but it seemed to him that there was nowhere to go. Among the tattered remains of the couch, the tattered roof shingles, Nick found a melted video game console. As he picked it up, he saw one of his models. A boat, his Viking ship, totally undamaged.

He reached for it and slipped. A nail went into his foot.

Nick howled.

Charlene climbed toward him. "Hold on to me," she said. "Stand up slowly, okay?"

His Viking ship

"I told you not to climb out there. What got into you?" His dad's voice sounded strange, strangled.

"Not now, Paul." Charlene pulled Nick up. He hung on to the boat, not caring about the pain in his leg. "He's going to need a tetanus shot."

"He's got to be careful!" His dad looked around, but Nick wasn't sure what he was looking for.

"Chill out, Dad," Jules said.

"I'm not going to *chill out*," their dad yelled. "Nicholas has been acting out ever since Charlene and Laurie moved in, and I have had enough."

With Charlene's help, Nick managed to get back to the grass. He pulled off the flip-flop and looked at the blood on his foot. It was too smeared for him to see where the nail had gone in.

"Nicholas," his father demanded, "what do you have to say for yourself?"

"Nothing," he said. "You don't want me to feel anything or think anything, anyway. I'm just supposed to do whatever you say."

"That's not true, Nicholas," his father said. "That's not fair."

"It is true. All you care about is your stupid development and your new marriage—you don't care about the past! You don't care—"

"Nicholas!" his father said, and Nick went silent.

Laurie stared at the wreckage of the house. Her eyes shone with water.

"Don't cry," Nick told her, and all of a sudden he was afraid he was going to cry too. "Don't be such a baby," he said, clenching his jaw. "You never even really lived there."

The look of shock and hurt she gave him was enough to drive back his own tears.

Cindy was holding his key ring.

Chapter Seven

IN WHICH Nick Dances to a New Tune

Back at the hotel Nick choked down a piece of rubbery pizza sitting on the king-sized bed in the grown-ups' room. His foot was freshly bandaged by a nurse at the doctor's office, and his arm was still stinging from the tetanus shot (it turned out he was due for a booster).

Lying on the scratchy coverlet, listening to the newscaster on the television announce that three fires had broken out in neighboring areas, Nick felt about as bad as he could imagine feeling. His dad watched the screen and chewed mechanically, ignoring the things they'd said before.

If life were more like the movies, they would have had a long talk and gotten closer or something. Instead, awkward tension hung, heavy and terrible, over Nick, making him wish he'd never spoken in the first place. But the boat was safe, and that was worth any amount of his dad's displeasure.

A knock on the door made him turn. Jules sprang up and let his girlfriend, Cindy, into the room.

"Hey," she said with an awkward wave.

"Our room is over there," Jules said. They walked through the dividing door, and a moment later the television switched on.

Charlene and Nick's father exchanged a glance.

"Why don't you two go watch television

with Jules," he said. "Keep them company."

Laurie shrugged, picked up another slice of pizza, and headed for the other room. Nick followed, not looking at his dad.

Jules and Cindy were crouched in the bathroom, and Cindy was holding his key ring.

"What are you doing?" Nick said, his voice going shrill as a scream.

"Hey, keep it down," said Jules. "I'm showing her the hobgoblin thing. What did you think I was doing?"

"Amazing," Cindy said. "Wow. You guys caught that?"

Laurie frowned. Clearly, in giving Jules the Sight she hadn't realized that he was going to act like he owned it. Clearly, she'd never had an older brother.

"Laurie caught it," Nick said.

Laurie crouched down and fed Sandspur a

chunk of her pizza. He devoured it in a single swallow and then looked at her expectantly. The leash that attached him to the pipes looked pretty well gnawed, so maybe he'd gotten hungry.

"Did you tell her the part where we're all going to die?" Nick asked.

"Not yet," said Jules.

"What?" asked Cindy.

Jules sighed. "Nick and Laurie say that basically, well, there are giants, and the giants are going to burn everything the way they burned Mangrove Hollow."

"That's crazy," Cindy said.

"It was on the news," Laurie said.

"Giants were on the news?"

"No," said Laurie, "things burning were on the news. More and more things burning."

"You know the story about the Pied Piper?" Nick asked. "Maybe this is far-fetched, but

what if we could lure the giants with singing?"
Maybe if they had Taloa around, it would have
been a better plan, but he was glad that she'd
left before everything had been destroyed. He
was glad that she was probably safe.

And, anyway, they needed something that
could swim in the sea. Leading the giants away
from the development wasn't going to be enough
anymore.

"That story didn't end
well," Laurie said.

"Lure the giants?
Lure them where?"
asked Jules.

"Where were
you when

you saw the mermaid?" he asked his brother.

"Why?" Jules asked.

"The nixie's song lured a giant, so merfolk singing should work even better. If we lure the giants into the ocean, then they won't be able to burn anything. No one will be in danger, and then maybe after a swim the giants'll go back to sleep. We just need the merfolk to help us." He grinned as he said it. He wasn't good with fighting and he wasn't all that brave, but he could figure things out. Tab A into slot B. It made sense. It was just crazy.

"Okay, hold on, genius. Where are they going to go? Out to sea? And then just drown like rats or something?"

"According to this field guide we have, sometimes they live underwater for long periods of time," Nick said. "They'd probably survive."

"So what good is the plan if they don't die?"

"Well, as long as one of the mermaids kept

singing, they'd probably just listen. And after a while they go back to hibernating. Plus, if they get lost out there in the ocean, it might take time for them to find their way back . . . enough time for us to think of something else."

"The things I saw didn't look helpful," Jules said. "Those mermaids or whatever. I think they tried to drown me."

"It's a good plan," said Laurie. "Maybe the mermaids felt threatened. Maybe your surfboard looked like a shark?"

"That's stupid," said Nick.

"I was defending you!"

"Look," Jules said, "asking homicidal or neurotic or *stupid* mermaids for help—I don't think you can call that a good plan. But I guess it's our only plan. It can't hurt to try."

"Now?" Laurie said.

"I'll drive," said Jules.

Laurie slung her bag over her shoulder,

opened the door, and looked out into the hall. "Come on. Bring Sandspur."

Jules locked the door between the rooms quietly and then followed her. Nick untied the hobgoblin's leash and led him along behind them.

"They're going to hear the car," said Nick. "What with the bumper dragging."

Jules looked up at the dark hotel, sighed, and clicked the button on his keys that would unlock their father's shiny new SUV. "We can take Dad's if we're quick."

There were two beaches in town. One was on the shore of the estuary, where little kids would play in the gentle waves, but the other one was over the bridge to the strip of land that met the Atlantic. That was the place for serious surfers.

Jagged sea-sculpted stones jutted from the sand in strange configurations so that the sea splashed up through the gaps, giving it the name Roaring Rocks. In the darkness sand whistled across the beach.

"Now what?" Jules asked.

Cindy pulled her zipped hoodie tighter around herself. "Are you guys messing with me?"

"What if I got in the water?" Nick asked. "I could call to them."

Jules laughed. "Can you even swim?"

Nick frowned.

"Of course he can," Cindy said, walking over to him. "Right, Nick?"

"I swim," he said as firmly as he could, grateful for Cindy's warm hand on his shoulder. He didn't want to admit that going out alone into that dark water seemed about the worst idea he could imagine. He tried not to think about how sharks often feed close to shore at night, riding the waves with their mouths agape. Not that merfolk were much better.

He waded out, saltwater stinging the cut on his foot. "Please," he called, "people of the sea. Um, we know you're there. Please help us."

"Hey," Laurie said, pointing. "Look there."

On a rock outcropping with waves breaking over it, dark shapes slid into the water.

"What?" Cindy asked, but they ignored her, watching as things moved among the waves, things that might just have been the shock of white foam, a clump of seaweed, a piece of driftwood carried along by the current to crash against the shore.

Then heads bobbed to the surface, dark

shapes on the waves. Like a school of fish, they turned at once toward the shore. Their hair was long and dark with wetness. Their eyes were pale as the moon.

"*You called to us*," they said.

"We need your help," Nick said.

"*Land and sea are no allies. You steal from us. You upset the balance. We would steal from you in return.*"

Nick tried to understand their words, to pick apart the strange music of their voices. They didn't sing, like Taloa, but the chorus of their voices sounded like song. "If you could just sing, really *sing*, you could lead giants to the water."

"You called to us."

"Why would we do that, dry dweller?"

"They're burning the land." Nick hesitated. "They can't burn the ocean."

"Who are you talking to?" Cindy asked. Her voice sounded too high, scared.

"Take her hand," Laurie told Jules.

Nick looked back and saw his brother slide his hand into hers. She gasped, looking out at the waves, and jerked her fingers out of his grip. A moment later she hesitantly took his hand again.

"You're doing great," Jules called to him. "Keep talking."

"We care nothing for your burning land. It must die to be reborn. It must be washed clean with fire. That is how it is and how it must be."

"Can we give you something back?" Laurie called. "Something we've stolen? Would that make you help us?"

Nick thought of a program he'd seen on

sharks and how their fins were being turned into soup and how dolphins were getting tangled in the plastic netting that holds soda cans together. He wasn't sure they could give anything back that the mermaids might want.

"*Give us something new,*" they said. "*Bring us a new fish. A fish that has never swum in our sea, a new fish for all of what you have taken.*"

"But we can't create a new fish!" Nick said.

The merfolk swam closer, surrounding Nick. He looked back at the shore again and Jules dropped Cindy's hand. He dropped his keys in the sand and started running toward the sea.

"Wait," Laurie called to Jules, but he wasn't paying attention. She followed him to the edge of the waves and spoke to the merfolk instead. "So if we bring you a fish that you've never seen, one that's never been in your sea, you'll sing for us?"

"*Yes,*" they said as one.

Jules waded out toward Nick, but a few merfolk swam between the two of them.

Nick swallowed hard. "What if we can't?" he couldn't stop himself from asking.

MERMAID

He expected wet hands to close on his arms, but it was Jules they grabbed. Three mermaids fastened their long fingers on his legs and unbalanced him. He fell into the waves and disappeared below them.

"We will take this one. Our theft from the land. Bring us a new fish by dawn or forfeit him forever to the sea.

"And burn," they said, and turned as one to splash deep into the sea.

They sat in the car with the windows rolled up and the doors locked, Cindy in the driver's seat, clutching the key ring. "Did I really see that?" she kept repeating. And then, "I really saw that."

"We have until dawn," said Laurie. Beside her, even Sandspur was still and grave.

"He was just standing in the water," Cindy said. "He just stood there and then he was gone."

"They took him," Nick said.

"I saw him go under. Under the waves. Like he's drowning and we're just driving away instead of saving him."

"We are saving him," Laurie said. "We're going to save him."

Nick turned to Laurie. "You shouldn't have said that thing about giving them something from the land. That's what gave them the idea. These things aren't Tinker Bell! You have to stop trusting them!"

"I know that," Laurie said, but her hand was touching the head of the hobgoblin as she said it.

Tab A into slot B. Nick had to think of a good idea. They had until dawn to get a new fish.

"Okay, so where are we going?" Cindy asked, her hand on the wheel.

"We have to find a fish," Nick said. "A fish that doesn't exist yet." Cindy's eyes widened. "We'll figure it out," he amended quickly.

"What about a plastic fish?" Laurie said. "Or what if we dyed a regular goldfish blue or something?"

"Can you even dye a fish a color?" Nick asked.

She shrugged. "And have it live?"

"They don't want a dead fish!" he said.

"Okay! I don't know!"

He pressed his fingers to his forehead, hoping that he could make himself have an idea. He had to focus. A new fish. A fish that had never swum in their sea. A fish new to their sea.

"Wait," Nick said. "What sea?"

"What?" Cindy asked.

He thought about the geography he'd studied the past year. There were lots of seas — even landlocked ones like the Dead Sea and the Caspian Sea. No way would mermaids here know of fish there. He turned to Cindy. "We need to get a fish that's from a different sea."

Cindy frowned, but Nick thought she was just having a hard time getting used to the idea that mermaids were real. He knew how she felt.

"But how would that help?" Laurie asked. "All the fish in it are from the ocean. Obviously."

"Well, yeah, but not necessarily *this* sea—the Atlantic. There are lots of different oceans, and some of them are warm like this one and probably pH-balanced pretty close but have fish they've never seen because they don't migrate there. Like, say, the Pacific or Indian oceans."

"How do you know the mermaids don't migrate there?"

"I don't!" Nick said. "But there are landlocked seas. How could they?"

Cindy gave him a surprised look. "Hey, that's smart."

Nick tried not to feel

too insulted. "Now we just have to figure out how to get one."

"That's not a problem," she said. "My dad has a fish tank. A big fancy saltwater one."

Nick wanted to hug her. "Do you know what you have in the tank?"

"The official names of them?" Cindy shook her head. "No, but my dad does."

Cindy's house was a ranch with a lime green mailbox and pink bougainvillea draped over the entrance. Nick had a horrible image of what the house would look like after a fire.

"My father is so in love with those fish, he's named each one," she said as they got closer to the door. "We're going to get Jules back, right?"

Nick nodded because he wasn't good at lying

out loud. He hoped they would get Jules back; he hoped this would work.

Laurie cradled Sandspur in her arms.

"What are you bringing him for?" Nick asked.

"He's chewed most of the way through his leash," she said. "I'm afraid he'll get away if I leave him in the car."

"Nick," Cindy said, "you are in charge of asking my dad about the fish. And Laurie, you have to get that thing out of there while my dad is distracted."

"What do you do?" Nick asked.

"Drive the getaway car and get grounded for the rest of my life," she said, and opened the door.

Both her parents were sitting on the couch in front of the television. Fires raged across the screen. Cindy's parents looked up when she came in, but Nick's gaze was drawn to the enormous tank that divided the living room from the kitchen.

"Good, you're home, Cindy! Is Jules all right? We've been watching the news—"

"We're in a hotel," Nick said, thinking of Jules lost under the waves. "Everybody's fine."

"This is Jules's brother, Nick, and his sister, Laurie."

"Isn't it a little bit late for you two?"

"Can I use your bathroom?" Laurie asked, and when they nodded, she slunk off.

Cindy sat on the edge of the sofa, blocking the view of the giant tank. She said something, but Nick wasn't paying attention. He was watching Laurie sneak toward the fish tank.

Cindy cleared her throat and he turned abruptly. "I was just telling my dad that you came in because you were interested in getting a tank yourself."

"Oh yeah," Nick said. "Yeah, I mean, I guess we have to get a house first, but . . ." He had no idea what to say. How did he get stuck talking? Laurie could have come up with some totally reasonable reason why she needed to know about the fish, but he had no idea what would be convincing.

Cindy glared at him, and he reminded himself that he had to get it together.

"But . . . ," he started again. "But I can catch local fish, so I was wondering which ones weren't local. I was hoping to try to trade a pet store local fish that I caught for ones from . . . from faraway places."

Nick looked over at Laurie, standing very close to the tank, with Sandspur balanced on one of her shoulders. Laurie gave him a thumbs-up.

"Well, it's a big responsibility to keep a saltwater tank," Cindy's dad said. "You have to check it regularly and be very careful. It isn't like keeping goldfish."

Nick nodded along and tried to look responsible.

"Well, that huge blue one with the yellow splotch is from pretty far away. My prize: George. He's come all the way from the Red Sea, haven't you, George? I've raised him ever since he was a little fish, and he just keeps growing." Cindy's dad shook his head as though still surprised by all that growing.

The Red Sea is mostly *landlocked*, Nick thought. He glanced toward Laurie and gave a slight nod.

Laurie reached under the huge cabinet and came up a few moments later with a net. Nick saw her out of the corner of his eye and hoped that no one else noticed. Cindy's dad started talking about another fish, this one named Clifford, who nearly died after being sucked into the filter, but

Nick barely heard him. He was so focused on not giving Laurie away that he couldn't concentrate on anything else.

He saw her climb up onto the edge of the cabinet and take a green vase from a nearby bookshelf. She dumped out the silk flowers under a chair and filled the vase with water from the tank while Cindy's dad talked on and her mother watched the television. Then she actually got the fish net and swept it around the tank. Water sloshed. The blue fish hid behind bright-colored coral splotched with algae.

"So, uh," Nick said, "what size tank is too small to start with?"

Cindy's dad opened his mouth to answer when the curtains across the room crashed to the floor, Sandspur tangled in them.

Cindy's mother jumped up. "How did . . ." Nick had a sinking feeling that Cindy's family didn't have a cat to blame.

Cindy's father stood up just as the blue fish flopped into the net.

"What the hell are you kids doing?" he yelled.

Laurie thrust the fish into the vase.

Nick grabbed for the curtains, sweeping the hobgoblin up in them.

"Go!" Cindy shouted. "Go!"

"Cindy!" her mother called as they ran out the door and hopped into the car. Cindy turned the key and hit the gas. As they drove away, Nick could see Cindy's parents in the road, still calling after them.

Cindy drove quietly, concentrating on the road. When her phone started to buzz, she turned it off without comment.

"I'm sorry," Laurie said for the millionth time. "I told you he'd almost chewed through the leash."

Nick wondered how they were going to explain this to any of their parents. Did Cindy's mom have his dad's number? Probably. It was only a matter of minutes before he realized that they were gone and his car was missing.

The hobgoblin thrashed in the curtains, biting and scratching and howling. The fish stared from the vase, its eyes enlarged by the curved glass until they seemed impossibly huge. Trapped. Just like Nick.

He frowned and reached into his bag, looking through what he had there. He had to be prepared, like the field guide said, like Jared had been. Then he realized what he needed.

"Laurie," he said, "can I see your bag?"

"Go!" Cindy shouted.

They left the hobgoblin biting one of the leather seats and walked down the beach. Nick could barely contain his nerves.

Laurie held up the vase and took Cindy's hand. "We brought you a fish," Laurie said.

At first nothing surfaced as waves crashed against the shore, but then three mermaids surfaced. *"The others have gone to feed,"* they said in unison.

"Here, look." Laurie walked toward the mermaids, her feet splashing through the waves.

Nick ran toward her. "Be careful."

"Now give us back Jules. Give us Nick's brother!"

One of them reached down and drew Jules up. He looked dazed. He didn't swim toward them.

Cindy waded out through the waves past Laurie and grabbed hold of Jules. Slinging his arm over her shoulders, she dragged him back to shore.

One of the mermaids peered curiously over the lid. Her eyes widened, and then she made a shrill sound. Merfolk leaped from the sea, splashing toward her. They all peered at the blue fish.

"You have to acclimate the fish first," Laurie warned. "Let the vase float for a few minutes."

"*He's beautiful,*" one of them said, and they sighed, all together.

"*I have never seen a fish like him,*" another said.

"*I saw a similar fish once . . . ,*" another began. "*But it was smaller and had red markings and a bigger mouth.*"

"*How could there be a new fish? A fish we have never seen?*" they all lamented at once. "*How could you have finished a fool's errand?*"

"You agreed to help us," Laurie said. "We let you keep one of us as a hostage, but now you have to help us. You have to sing."

One of the mermaids took the vase, and

"He's beautiful".

another swam forward, toward them. A necklace of shells, coral, and bottle caps hung around her neck.

"*Very well,*" she said. And they began to sing.

Nick fumbled in his pocket.

Their song rose, beautiful and terrible, to echo in his ears. It was the sound of waves crashing on the shore. It was the sound of water beating against rocks, of a maelstrom, of a serene and peaceful sea. It was all those things together, and it mesmerized them.

Then, as abruptly as it began, it was over. Nick was surprised to find tears in his eyes.

"*Our debt is paid,*" they said. "*Now we go.*"

"Wait," Laurie said. "You said that you would help us!"

"*We said that we would sing for you. Now we have sung.*" With that, they sank slowly into the sea, taking the fish and the vase with them.

"No! You can't!" Laurie screamed after them, but they were gone.

She sat down in the sand and stared at where they had been. Jules groaned loudly. Nick only smiled.

"What's your problem?" Jules asked him. "What are you smiling about?"

Nick reached into his pocket and took out Laurie's microcassette recorder, which he'd taken from her bag, and hit play. The sound of mermaids singing was a little scratchy, but compelling all the same.

"Didn't you *read* that book?" Nick said to Laurie. "You never trust faeries."

Jules clapped Nick on the back, and Laurie laughed. "You are a genius," he said. "A total crazy genius."

"Now what do we do?" Cindy asked.

Nick stopped smiling.

"You are a genius."

"I know lots."

Chapter Eight

IN WHICH a Bridge Is Crossed

Jules was able to walk to the car, and he looked like he was fine, but Nick remembered his dazed look when he'd been pulled from under the waves, and he worried.

"What was it like?" Cindy asked. "Was it like that movie where crabs sing and there's a big palace under the waves?"

"Not really," Jules said, avoiding meeting her gaze.

"How are we even going to find the giants?" Laurie asked.

"I don't know," Nick said.

"Well, it was good to have a plan while it lasted," Cindy said. "Maybe our new plan can be to run."

Nick looked into the backseat, where Sandspur squatted, eating some pieces of lint he'd found on the floor mats. "He told me that he avoids giants' territories. That means he knows where they are," Nick said.

"I know lots," said the little faerie.

"What if we let you go once you show us?"

"No!" said Laurie. "Not Sandzy! I want to keep him! I want him to be our friend!"

"Laurie," Jules said, and Laurie sighed.

"Okay," Laurie said, and the hobgoblin stuck out his tongue at her. "Okay, fine. But only if this works."

"You'll let me go?" asked the little creature.

"Yeah," said Laurie.

"And you'll feed me first?" he said.

"Sure," said Jules quickly. "Whatever you want."

"Whatever I want?" His eyes got wide. "I want! I want!"

"Don't promise him *any*thing! Are you crazy?" Nick said, but it was too late. He had no idea what the little faerie was going to ask Jules for, but he was glad they wouldn't have to deal

with that until after everything else. If they could really rid Florida of its giant problem, they could figure out a way around any crazy demand.

"So, okay," Jules said. "I rig up some speakers, we blast this recording, drive around, get giants to follow us, and then what? We drive to the water . . . but what happens after that?"

"Uh . . . ," Nick said. "We drive into the water like in a movie? We jump out of the car and let it roll on out."

"We'd die," Laurie said.

Cindy nodded. "We'd totally bite it."

"Even if we swim for it, Nick, how far is the car realistically going to roll?" Jules asked. "A few feet? Then we have until the battery on the recorder runs out, and the giants will be back in business."

Nick groaned. His plan had seemed so simple before, but now it felt hopelessly complex. "At least they'll be in one place. Maybe they'll fight for territory there and kill one another. That would be something, right?"

"That seems like it would be totally destructive. Like, apocalyptic," Cindy said.

"I don't know," Nick said, defeated. "Maybe we should call Jared. Or Jack."

"It's the middle of the night. We're on our own. The minute we go back, we're all grounded forever." Laurie sighed again. "Just think."

"Well, we need something. Something that can keep—" Nick stopped speaking as he thought of it. The boat. The boat his mother had given him, the only thing of his that had survived the wreckage of the house. But as he thought of it, he was afraid to say it out loud. It could work, they could tape the recorder down and send it out to sea, but the boat would be gone forever. He didn't want to give it up. He didn't want to let go of the past, to see it sail across the water and sink below the horizon. He wasn't ready for finality.

"What?" Laurie asked. "You look like you've got an idea."

"Never mind," he said. "I don't know if it would work, anyway."

They all were silent for a moment, and then Nick said, "We would have to go back to the hotel. Get something out of the room. And that's impossible, right?"

Jules scratched his head. "What do you need?"

"The boat," Nick said quietly. "That boat I built. The remote control is gone, but if I turn the engine on, the boat can still travel in a straight line. We could rig it up and release it. The giants would follow it out into the ocean. They'd be so far out by the time it ran out of juice that who knows how long it would take for them to find their way back."

Jules was nodding. "That could work."

Laurie frowned, but not like she was disagreeing. Like she was considering. "What about the tide?"

"High tide's at about five in the morning," Cindy said. "Anytime after that it'll be going back out. We'd have to stay up all night."

"It's going to take us all night anyway," Laurie said. "To get the giants."

"The water will be real glassy that time of day," said Jules. "Which is good. One big wave could take your boat out."

"I know this is my plan," Nick said, "but maybe it's a bad idea."

"If we don't do this, what happens?" asked Jules.

None of them answered. Nick thought of fire.

"So we do it," Jules said, slinging his arm around Nick's shoulders. "And we hope for the best."

They pulled up across the street from the hotel, and Jules took out his cell phone.

"You sure about this?" Laurie asked.

"Yeah," said Jules. "He'll be so busy yelling at me there's no way he'll hear you. Go!"

Jules's face looked pale, and Nick knew how much he'd avoided being in trouble, avoided a confrontation like this. Jules flipped open the cell and scrolled to the number. There was a long pause.

"We're just hanging out," Jules said into the phone.

Cindy waved at them to get going.

"Bring me a doughnut," the hobgoblin squeaked from the backseat. "Or crackers. Yes, doughnut crackers!"

Nick and Laurie scrambled out of the backseat. They used the key card to open the side door of the hotel and ran up the stairs. Listening against the wall, Nick could hear his father shouting into the phone.

"Just tell me where you are! Is your brother

with you? Laurie? You know that I almost reported my car as stolen? Do you know that?"

Nick slid the card into the lock and pushed open the door. He didn't want to take a chance on the door closing, so he just held it open and pointed to the boat. Laurie ran across the room and picked it up.

As they headed back down the hall, Nick heard his dad yell, "If you don't tell me where you are right now, I am going to call the police!"

Then the elevator chimed, they jumped in it, and the hallway and their parents were gone.

It took Jules about an hour to duct tape a portable stereo to the top of the car and rig it so it could play the microcassette. It involved some cutting of wires and electrical tape that he

The elevator chimed.

bought from an all-night gas station convenience store, plus the standard cassette adapter from Laurie's bag. And if Jules sometimes looked off into the distance and needed to be shoved by Cindy to get back to the task, well, Nick hoped that was only because Jules was tired.

"Okay," Cindy said finally, coming over to where Laurie and Nick were taking turns throwing cheese-covered popcorn to Sandspur every time he marked down a new giant on a big glossy map.

"We have a route," Nick said. "Most of the places aren't even that far. It's maybe a thirty-mile radius."

"Jack said the highest concentration of giants was in this area." Laurie threw another piece of popcorn in the hobgoblin's direction, and he scuttled for it, trailing the twine she'd bought to release him.

"If we start now, we should get back here just after the tide starts going out. The sun will just be coming up."

"At least no one's on the roads this late."

Jules started up the car and they got in. Cindy drank a large cup of coffee like it was water. "Is this the dumbest thing we've ever done?" she asked him.

"This is totally the dumbest thing we've ever done," said Jules.

"Just checking," she said, and turned on the stereo.

Nick and Laurie climbed in the back.

"It is totally ridiculous that this could save Florida," Jules told him, "but good job thinking it up."

Nick grinned. "Just drive like you're playing a video game."

Jules smiled back at him and tousled his hair.

"Maybe you should be the one driving, then."

It was strange, how happy Nick felt. He was still scared, but he was excited, too.

For almost an hour they followed the route on the map and nothing happened. They just drove through the darkness with the eerie sound of mermaid song drifting behind them.

"Did he just give you those coordinates to get food?" Jules asked.

"No!" said the hobgoblin. "I am good and honest! And hungry!"

Then they heard a heavy thudding sound as three giants leaped onto the road. Nick screamed so loudly that his throat hurt. Jules lost control of the car, swerving onto the side of the road, and then grabbed the wheel, jerking it hard. They passed the giant on the left so closely that Nick could have leaned out the window and brushed one massive, wrinkled, craggy

leg. He turned to look behind them. The giants chased them, running like rolling boulders.

"Drive!" screamed Laurie.

"Stick to the route!" yelled Nick. "It's working!"

They drove faster, taking the turns outlined on the map, giants following them in a growing horde. Sometimes Nick saw them shove one another as more and more burst from the woods and came pushing from the ground and cracking through the asphalt. More than ten, then more than twenty, then more than Jack's anticipated thirty.

A crowd of giants roaring toward them.

"We're almost there," Cindy said. "I can see the water."

The car pulled onto the bridge right after the

exit to the estuary beach, and Nick looked out at the glittering lights along the shore. The thudding of his heart and the footsteps of the giants seemed to be beating together, thundering faster and faster as the car accelerated . . .

. . . and then stopped short, Jules slamming his hands against the wheel. He screamed with frustration.

"Jules!" Nick leaned forward. "What are you doing?"

Up ahead of them, a horn started blaring and the sides of the bridge began to rise. The barrier bars were already down and a sailboat with two tall masts glided toward the opening in the bridge.

"I couldn't make it across in time," Jules said. He sounded numb.

"No, no, no, no," Cindy said, looking back. There were no other cars. At least they could be glad about that.

Nick grabbed hold of his little Viking ship with the microcassette recorder taped to it, opened the door of the car, and climbed out into the street. He could hear the giants pounding toward him, like rocks crashing down a hill, but he couldn't think about that.

"Nick!" Laurie yelled, and he remembered his dad yelling for him when he was walking through the debris. He couldn't think about that, either.

He jumped up on the hood of the car and pulled out the tiny tape from the stereo, knocking off the adapter. Everything went quiet for a moment except for the thudding of massive feet and the slap of the waves. Shoving the tape into the boat, he hit the play button.

The mermaids sang again, grainy now, and softer, but at the highest volume the recorder could supply. It didn't seem like it could possibly be enough.

A giant reached for Nick. He dodged and nearly tripped. Earth dusted the ground, and the smell of roots and minerals overwhelmed everything else.

Nick sprinted toward the side of the bridge and raced up it along the bike path as the incline got steeper, the bridge rising farther and farther up. He came up short at the railings. The boat slid in his sweaty hands as he flipped the switch that turned on the motor and the engine whirred to life.

Please, he thought as he leaned as far as he could over the side. *Please. Please let this work. Please don't let us die.*

He turned the boat in what he hoped was the right position and dropped it over the side of the bridge. It streaked down, the song falling and then disappearing as the boat went under the waves.

The giants roared behind him. Cracks

Please let this work.

spiderwebbed out from where the giants stepped, and overhead a stay snapped. Nick wasn't sure how much longer the bridge could hold their weight.

He closed his eyes.

Then Nick heard the song again, rising up. The water seemed to amplify the noise; it was strong, beautiful, loud. He looked down and saw the little Viking ship bobbing its way out to the sea. Its prow was pointed at the horizon, and the boat moved steadily along toward it.

The giants roared with anguish. One shredded the stays to throw itself off the side of the bridge. Others charged toward the ravine and hurled themselves into the ocean.

Nick slumped down as the bridge began to close and noticed for the first time that Cindy and Jules and Laurie were already out of the car. Jules had a tire iron in one hand and his key ring in the other.

"We're okay," Nick said. "Everything's okay now. Everything's going to be okay."

Jules rested his hand against Nick's shoulder, and Laurie reached out to pull Nick up.

As the sun rose, bathing the water in gold, they watched the heads of the giants sink lower and lower and finally disappear into the horizon.

"What are you doing here?"

Chapter Nine

IN WHICH the World Turns
Upside Down Again

Nick, Laurie, Cindy, and Jules ate pancakes drenched in syrup and drank as many cups of orange juice as they could hold. Every bite bought them another moment before they got in the worst trouble of their lives.

Finally, yawning, they dropped Cindy off at her house and headed to the hotel.

Jules cut the engine halfway down the block and steered the car into a parking space with the momentum. Everything was still and wet with dew when they got out.

Sitting on the steps were Jared, Simon, and Mallory.

"What are you doing here?" Nick whispered, looking up at the windows of the building.

Mallory stood up. She looked older than he had expected, and her hair had been cut into a short bob, but she still looked like the drawings of her. "You must be Nick. We found out something about the giants."

"What?" asked Laurie.

"One of the pages I took with me," Jared said. "It helped explain some other papers we'd seen before but didn't understand. It looks like the reason the giants wake up is to kill something else. Something worse."

Nick looked over at Laurie. She hugged Sandspur to her chest. Even Jules, who had no idea who these kids were, said nothing.

Nick had thought he'd saved the world, but instead he'd doomed it.

End of
BOOK TWO

About TONY DiTERLIZZI . . .

Tony DiTerlizzi is the author and illustrator of *Jimmy Zangwow's Out-of-This-World Moon-Pie Adventure*, as well as the Zena Sutherland Award–winning *Ted*. In 2003, his brilliantly cinematic version of Mary Howitt's classic poem "The Spider and the Fly" received stellar reviews, earned Tony his second Zena Sutherland Award, and was honored as a Caldecott Honor Book. His most recent picture book is *G Is for One Gzonk!*, and his most recent novel is *Kenny & the Dragon*, his first chapter book. Tony's art has also graced the work of such well-known fantasy names as J. R. R. Tolkien, Anne McCaffrey, Peter S. Beagle, and Jane Yolen as well as Wizards of the Coast's *Magic: The Gathering*. He, his wife, and his daughter reside in Amherst, Massachusetts. Visit Tony at www.diterlizzi.com.

and HOLLY BLACK

Holly Black's first novel, *Tithe: A Modern Faerie Tale*, was published in the fall of 2002. It was a YALSA Best Book for Young Adults and made YALSA's Teens' Top Ten booklist for 2003. A companion novel, *Valiant: A Modern Tale of Faerie*, won the Andre Norton Award for young adult fiction from the Science Fiction and Fantasy Writers of America. Her most recent solo venture is a *New York Times* bestselling companion to *Tithe* and *Valiant* entitled *Ironside: A Modern Faery's Tale*. She has also contributed to anthologies by Terri Windling, Ellen Datlow, and Tamora Pierce. Holly also lives in Amherst, Massachusetts. She lives with her husband, Theo, and a remarkable menagerie. Visit Holly at www.blackholly.com.

Because the cycle
has been broken,
greater peril
has awoken.

Only with the
help of friends
can nature be made
right again.

Our giant friends—
please call them home.
The seas are not
their place to roam.

GIANT

They are needed
here on land
to quell a furor
close at hand.

And water friends—
merrow, nixie—
capricious, cruel,
and oh so trickſy,

NIXIE

must be convinced
to put away
their malice till
another day

and work alongside
human friends—
since their fates,
entwined, depend

THE VARGAS KIDS

on finding many
happy ends.

THE WYRM KING
BOOK THREE OF THREE

BOOKS BY

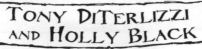

TONY DiTERLIZZI
AND HOLLY BLACK

ACKNOWLEDGMENTS

Tony and Holly would like to thank
Kevin, our faithful, fantastical guide
for this grand adventure,
Linda, for mapping out Mangrove Hollow
(and the spaghetti!),
Cassie, Cecil, Kelly, and Steve,
for their smarts,
Barry, for all his help,
Ellen, Julie, and all the folks at Gotham,
Will, for keeping Tony on track,
Theo, for all the patience and encouragement,
Angela (and Sophia) — more Spiderwick!
More endless nights of discussion!
At least it was on a beautiful, sunny Florida beach . . .

and all the wonderfully talented folks at S&S for
all of their support in bringing the next chapter
in the Spiderwick tale to life.